This
Treasure Cove Story
belongs to

D0586556

INCREDIBLES 2

A CENTUM BOOK 978-1-912396-91-7
Published in Great Britain by Centum Books Ltd.
This edition published 2018.

1 3 5 7 9 10 8 6 4 2

© 2018 Disney Enterprises, Inc. and Pixar. All Rights Reserved.

No part of this publication may be reproduced, stored in a retrieval
system, or transmitted in any form or by any means, electronic,
mechanical, photocopying, recording or otherwise without
the prior permission of the publishers.

Centum Books Ltd, 20 Devon Square, Newton Abbot,
Devon, TQ12 2HR, UK.

www.centumbooksltd.co.uk | books@centumbooksltd.co.uk
CENTUM BOOKS Limited Reg. No. 07641486.

A CIP catalogue record for this book is available
from the British Library.

Printed in China.

A Treasure Cove Story

DISNEY · PIXAR

INCREDIBLES 2

Adapted by
SUZANNE FRANCIS

Illustrated by
SATOSHI HASHIMOTO

Designed by
TONY FEJERAN

The Incredibles were a **FAMILY OF SUPERS**.
When a machine started ripping up the city, they
sprang into action! While Mr Incredible and Elastigirl
tried to stop it, their kids Violet and Dash grabbed baby
Jack-Jack. Their friend Frozone joined in the fight!

The Incredibles stopped the machine but got
in big trouble. Supers were not allowed to use their
powers. Mr Incredible and Elastigirl had no choice
but to return to their **UNDERCOVER LIVES**
as Bob and Helen Parr, along with their kids.

But then a wealthy businessman named Winston Deavor and his sister, Evelyn, proposed a plan to make Supers legal again. Elastigirl would get the first assignment. She was nervous, but this was her chance to help her family... **AND ALL SUPERS**.

I LOVE SUPERHEROES!

Winston was so excited to work with Elastigirl, he allowed her whole family to stay in one of his mansions. **DASH LOVED IT!** He used a remote control to move the floors and turn on the waterfalls.

On Elastigirl's first day at her new job, she spotted a runaway train! She hopped onto her Elasticycle and chased the train through the city.

She **SCRAMBLED** over rooftops...

... **ZOOMED** up a crane...

... and **ZIPPED** through a tunnel...

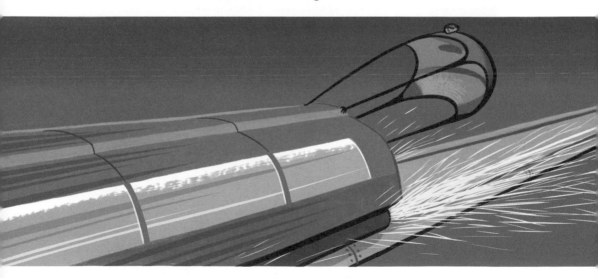

... until finally, she **STRETCHED** into a parachute
and slowed down the train – right before it ran
off the tracks!

Back at home, Bob was exhausted. Helping
with homework, changing nappies and dealing with
teenage drama really knocked him out.
    While Bob was napping, Jack-Jack watched TV.
Then he heard a **NOISE** in the backyard.

It was an intruder! Jack-Jack tried
to stop the criminal.

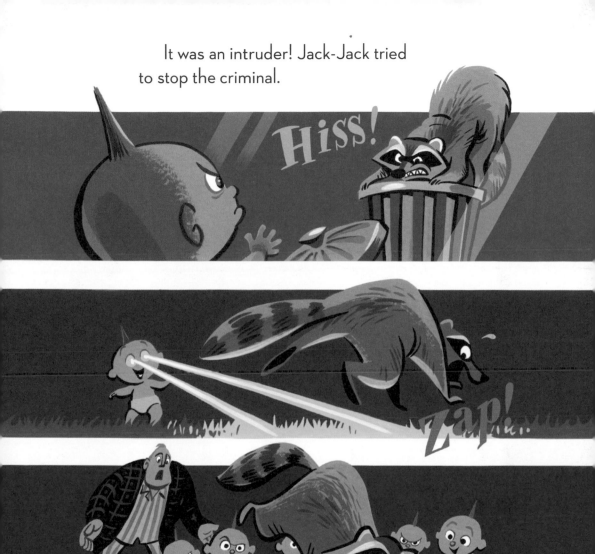

Bob heard the commotion and ran outside.
He couldn't believe his eyes.
'You... have... **POWERS**!'

The next day, the city buzzed with the news of Elastigirl's amazing rescue. During her first TV interview, a super villain called the **SCREENSLAVER** attacked. He took over an ambassador's helicopter. Elastigirl raced off...

... and **RESCUED** the ambassador!

Elastigirl still needed to catch the Screenslaver.
With Evelyn's help, she traced the villain's signal to
his lair. She chased him through the building and
CAPTURED him!

But something didn't feel right. Elastigirl realized she'd caught the wrong person – Evelyn Deavor was the *real* Screenslaver! Evelyn wanted to destroy her brother's plan and make sure Supers were never legal again. In a flash, Evelyn put **HYPNO-GOGGLES** on Elastigirl! She was under Evelyn's spell.

Meanwhile, Bob needed some serious help with Jack-Jack. The baby's powers were **UNCONTROLLABLE**!

Bob brought him to the smartest person he knew: Edna Mode. Edna made a special **SUPERSUIT** and tracker to help manage Jack-Jack's powers.

Everything was finally calm at home. Then Evelyn
called and said Elastigirl was in **TROUBLE**! Bob asked
Frozone to watch the kids and then rushed away.

When Mr Incredible arrived at the Deavors' ship,
a hypnotized Elastigirl pounced on him! She fought
him until she could put hypno-goggles over his eyes.

Meanwhile, a group of hypnotized Supers arrived
to capture the kids. Frozone showed up just in time to
help. Dash clicked a remote, and – **ZOOOOM!** – the
amazing **INCREDIBILE** pulled up! It whisked the kids
away while Frozone was captured by the Supers.

The Incredibile brought the kids to the ship. But where was Jack-Jack? Dash and Violet were tracking their lost brother when a hypnotized Super **ATTACKED**!

Violet flung razor-sharp force fields at the Super until she and Dash could escape.

Everyone on board was under Evelyn's
WICKED SPELL. She forced the Supers to
set the ship on a crash course towards the city.

Suddenly, the kids appeared. They **FREED**
their parents and Frozone from the hypnosis.
The family was ready to fight together!

The Incredibles and Frozone battled the rest of the hypnotized Supers. Before long, everyone was back to normal.

Then Evelyn tried to escape! Elastigirl chased after her. Evelyn was a **FIERCE OPPONENT**, but she was no match for Elastigirl.

All the Supers
**WORKED
TOGETHER**
to keep the ship from
crashing into the city
centre. They turned the
ship around, stopping
it just before it reached
the shore!

Everyone was grateful to the Supers. The city changed the law, making it legal for them to use their powers again.

Now the Incredibles were ready to face any challenge – **AS A FAMILY**!

Treasure Cove Stories

Book list may be subject to change.